THE LONG GOODBYE

Sami M. El-Soudani

The Long Goodbye by Sami M. El-Soudani

This book is written to provide information and motivation to readers. Its purpose is not to render any type of psychological, legal, or professional advice of any kind. The content is the sole opinion and expression of the author, and not necessarily that of the publisher.

Printed in the United States of America.

I WANT YOU
TO VOTE FOR AMERICA

LOS ANGELES EDITION

JSINESS

Los Angeles Times

JAMES FLANIGAN

Oil Runs Deep in U.S. Stance on Iraq

FLANIGAN: Development of Iraq's Oil Potential at Stake

On August 25th, 2002, that is about six months before the invasion of Iraq by the United States and Great Britain the Los Angeles Times published the article shown here, where a stock market financial analyst, James Flannigan set the record straight indicating that the real reason behind the invasion of Iraq is to gain control of its oil reserves.

Iraq is the world's second-largest oil reserves, but it's oil production lags behind that of many of the leading producers.

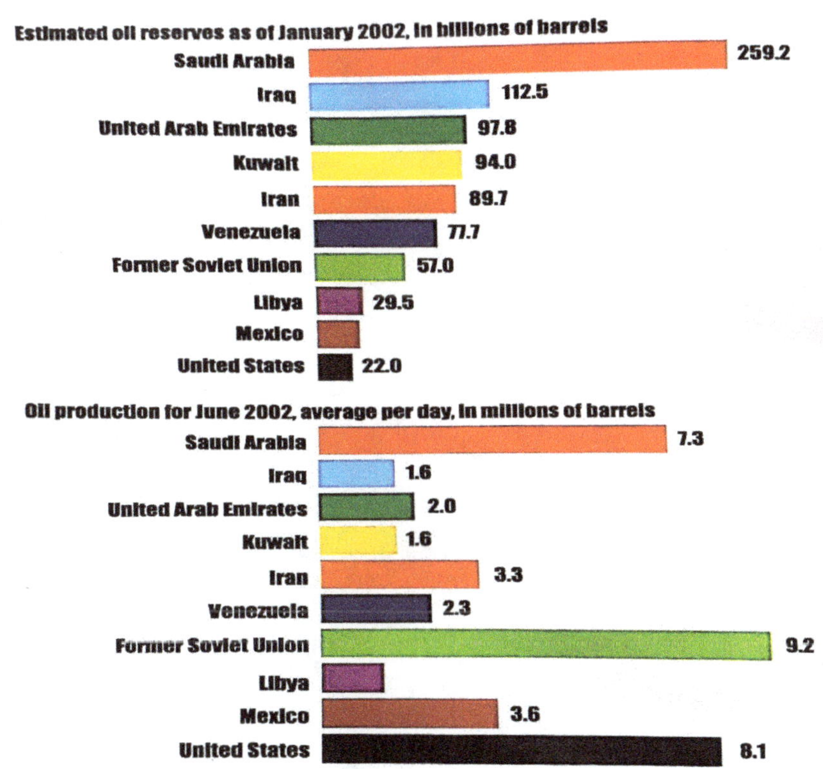

**Source: American Petroleum Institution,
World Oil/Los Angeles Times**

Data published by American Petroleum institute indicating that per most recent reliable estimates Iraq has the second largest crude oil reserves in the world. It appears that such findings may have intensified the interest in controlling the Iraqi government and possibly even accelerated the deposing of Saddam Hussein, replacing him with a more pliable regime, favorable to the heads of the "Virtual empire: Pax Ameritanica."

THE LONG GOOD-BYE

On the last day of the Long
Good-Bye
It felt like another Fourth of July
But what shall we really

Celebrate?
Six hundred thousand dead
Iraquis?
Or is it the opening of America's
prison gate?
Yet better late than never;
Yes Sir! There is a lesson here to relate
For all Americans to heed forever;

That was indeed a very long
Good-bye
With best wishes to you all
As today both Laura and I
Are moving back to Texas
To our everlasting glory

To a Presidential Library
With million copies of book
Telling my own story

President George W. Bush:
The Long Good-bye

1

There will be no such nonsense
About the two stolen elections

For it was sore losing Democrats
Who fabricated such fictions
But atop my greatest
accomplishments
Was hanging saddam Hussein
For Outlasting my Dad in Office

Causing him so much pain
It began with an embarrassment
In the media worldwide
To my Dad's disenchantment
Suffering the worst landslide
In America's election history
And boy! Was that a rough ride!

But my book will tell it all
In truth like Jesus' disciple
For upon retirement back to Texas
I took an oath on the Bible
That never again will I tell a lie

So for the Lord's sake don't you ever
ask me why?
It was my father out of the entire
American Nation
In conference with the Bin Ladens
in a southern State
From among six billion people of world population
Osama's brothers with a former U.S President on a
date?

United States 41st President George H. W. Bush lost his 1992 bid for the presidential re-election by a landslide, the largest in the United States history. This was in the wake of a major economic recession largely precipitated by his launching of the Guf war on Iraq in response to Iraq's President Saddam Hussein's Invasion and occupation of Kuwait in 1991.

What a Murphy's Law incredibly
suspicious situation!
And on the very day before September
eleven?
Was something going on behind the
back of our nation?
Or was it God's "Covert Operation"
blueprint in Heaven?
I must admit I am no believer in
Murphy's Law
But these coincidences strike me with awe
Yet no one asked the hard and honest
questions
Has there been any breaking
of the United States Law?

So please don't ask me why?
For I am under oath on the Bible
Never again will I tell a lie

With three thousand poor Americans
Murdered on the following day
thrusting our beloved nation into total disarray
And with me launching two wars on helpless nations
wreaking havoc worldwide, most grisly shall we say

Looking for terrorists we first went into Afghanistan
With well defined and unwavering military plan
To play hide-and-seek with Osama Bin Laden
An arch-terrorist a very illusive man

Osama Bin Laden,
a Very Illusive Man,
why is He Still at
Large, Escaping
Capture by the
United States?

Facing America with its
billion-dollar bombers
Playing our usual Texas-
style bounty hunters
But unable to capture Osama

Bin Laden
An arch-terrorist and a very
illusive man
Why couldn't we capture
Osama Bin laden?
Please don't ask me why?
For I am under oath on the
Bible
Never again will I tell a lie

Then we invaded prosperous Iraq,
With mighty firepower bringing it to blazes
And that was not to capture Iraqi oil wells
Or to build our fourteen huge military bases
Our sole-sourced Haliburton Contractor
Robbing our taxpayers obliged us by doing so
While Cheney and I were fixing to capture
Al-Qaeda's arch-terrorist Osama-on-the-go
But then why are we still dug in today,
In Iraq with fourteen huge military bases?

Please don't ask me why?
For I am under oath on the Bible
never again will I tell a lie

Dick Cheney and I
in search of Osama
Bin Laden; Our wan-
ton arch-terrorist,
also a very illusive
man; Why is he still
at large? Don't ask!

The United States Representatives Attending of the General Assembly of the United Nations Spreading Lies Abiut Iraq's Weapons of Mass Destruction (WMD), Based on False British Intelligence Reports. The United States CIA Director George Tenet Was Instructed to Sit Behind The U.S Secretary of State, Collin Powell for Enhanced Credibility, Despite the Fact That the U.S CIA had Privately Labeled the British Intelligence Reports as "Hoax" Per Representative Henry Waxman's Letter to President George W. Bush on 3/17/2003.

Behold! This is The Missing Law of Hammurabi. the King of Babylon: :Alas to my Servants! For They Know Not What is Heading Their Way on te Abraham Lincoln." With our Founding Fathers Turning Over in Their Graves in This twenty First Century, and With our New and Innovative Concepts of "Preemptive War" and "The Patriot Act," We Turn What was to be a Manageable "Fear of Terror" into an unconterollable and Totally Unimaginable "Terror of Fear." May God Bless America, and May God Also Save America, for We NowNeed that Latter Prayer for America More Than Ever Before in our Entire History…O' God Almighty Save us From our Greatest Enemy: Ourselves.

British Prime Minister Tony Blair, Better Known to US in America as Tony Brain, for He Delivered to the U.S. Preisident George W. Bush Sixteen Words of a British Intelligence Report, Which the U.S. President Used in His 2003 State-of-the-Union Address to the U.S. Congress , in Order to Justify the Invasion of Iraq on March 19,2003 by the United States of America and Great Britain. Here are Sixteen words of Wisdom: "The British Government Has Learned that Saddam Hussein Recently Sought Significant Quantities of Uranium from Africa."

Even Hitler would have cringed
at taking blame for such horror

But here I am, a man of courage
with unlimited capability
And don't ask me why Tony Blair
the mastermind of our terror
Remained reticent, as a cool Brit,
not sharing my gullibility

Please don't ask me why?
For I am under oath on the bible
Never again will I tell a lie

In 1992 my Dad left this Country
In a devastating recession,
Ending the twentieth Century
With a deficit progression

But that was magically reversed
As a recurring Republican obsession
By a Democratic President
Who happened to be in succession|
Leaving behind a projected ten-year tax surplus
A five-trillion-dollar national gift for all of us
But then I won the elections
And just like Dad like son
My eight years added more fun
As I let our beloved Country
In borderline depression
From both me and my Dad

Even Hitler would
have cringed at taking
blame for such horror

Allowing free wheeling arrests
As reminders now and then
And with Congress in addiction,
Nearly all members caved in
Defenders of the Constitution
Delirious, no longer recalling
America's precious Bill of Rights

Congressmen shaken by wiretapping!
With our Supreme Court flying kites
Yes! The U.S. Congress caved right in
Upon my sending of American
democracy
Once and forever on a tailspin
Thanks again to illegal
wiretapping
My best achievement of eight years
But how come no one is clapping?

Please don't ask me why?
for I am under oath on the Bible
Never again will I tell a lie

And my "axis of evil" was my simplest idea
So simple, I only had to count to three
That was Iran, Iraq, and North Korea,
But I kept a fourth ax just for me
My personal ax for self-defense
Against America's bully to be
A Venezuela rebel named Hugo Chavez

Venezuelan Leader Hugo Chavez Holding a book by Noam Chomsky Titled "Hegemony or Survival" in which the Eminent Author Criticized the Unjust United States Policy Towards Third-world Nations in General, and Towards Latin American Nations and the Middle East in Particular.

You should see him
launching his offense
Telling the whole world at the
United Nations
that he could clearly see
The Devil realized in me
And among all world nations
Only Americans are ruled by
Satans?
I cannot deny having used my ax
To carve "OPEC" in blood which made me relax
And then I chopped down OPEC's dreadful tree
Blood-for-oil for oil-addicted folks like you and me
So never mind wrestling Chavez in the mud
Let him keep buzzing at the United Nations
like a bee
But for the life of me why on earth
Do OPEC members hate us so much?

Please don't ask me why?
For I am under oath on the Bible
Never again will I tell a Lie

When the Israelis sent their American tanks roaring
Into Palestinian territory while totally ignoring
World anger over their inhumane barring
All news media from their war crime scene
while Israel's vicious army was totally destroying
The ill-fated Palestinian City of Jenin

Ariel Sharon,
Prime Minister
of Israel, "A
man of Peace"
in Conference
with the Long
Good-Bye

On that day if infamy I surely
sounded like a pro
When I ordered Ariel Sharon to
pull his tanks right back
But defiant Sharon decisively
told me where to go
Three days later I was softly
right back on the track
As I came round hopping with
my tail between my legs
I named Ariel Sharon, without a
doubt, "a man of peace"
As the tail was now wagging
the dog right off its four legs
For what good are allies for, if
they don't aim to please?
So Sharon, my man of peace,
turned Jenin into a cemetery
But that is Israel's affair;
no concern of mine or my country
For Ariel Sharon told me: George keep thinking "Roadmap"
And with that our precious alliance would never face a mishap
But then I was aware that Israel was building a horrible
wall
To secure illegal settlements besides those they wished to install
What a sinister plan tightening their noose on the poor
people of Palestine
A whole nation in prison with its people having no life
at all

The Apartheid Wall Built by
Israel Runs Hundred of Miles
Within the west Bank Territory
of Palestine Isolating the
United-Nations-Condemned
Illegal Israeli Settlements and
Creating Virtually Impossible
Working and Living Conditions
for the Palestinian Population
(Courtesy: Reuters' Photo

With three thousand poor Americans
Murdered on the following day
thrusting our beloved nation into total disarray
And with me launching two wars on helpless nations
Wreaking havoc worldwide, most grisly shall we say

And thus begins the third millennium of our Era …with a nightmare.

A heinous act for which there is no justification whatsoever, not in the Torah, not in the Bible, not in the Qur'an, in short, NOT IN THE BOOK. Humans tossing the Book behind their back, go for each other's throat instead. Only Godless people are capable of committing such a crime against humanity.

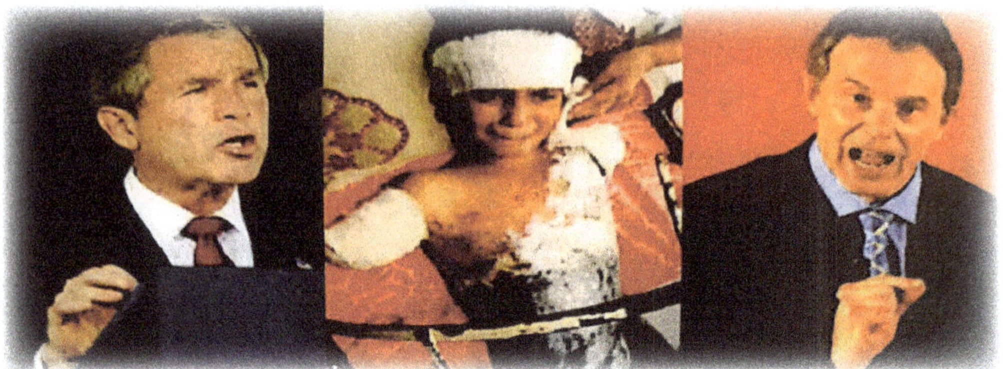

The U.S. 43rd President "The Long Good-Bye"

Ali Ismaeel Abbas: An Iraqi twelve-year-old child victim among the hundreds of thousands of victims of the United States and British Surgical Bombing Holocaust during Bushes' first and second gulf wars, invading Iraq by a coalition of the United States and British Armed Forces.

British Prime Minister Tony Brain

Here are the Infamous Sixteen Words Fed by Tony Brain to the Long Good-Bye and Plugged into The Long Good-Bye's State-of-the-Union Address to the United States Congress Indicating that the Invasion of Iraq is a Must for the Very Survival of the United States of America:

"The British Government has Learned that Saddam Hussein Recently Sought Significant Quantities of Uranium from Africa."

Cartoon Art Work Contribution by Nabawia Jane El-Soudani,
MFA, California Institute of the Arts

And my "axis of evil" was my simplest idea
So simple, I only had to count to three
That was Iran, Iraq, and North Korea,
But I kept a fourth ax just for me
My personal ax for self-defense
Against America's bully to be
A Venezuelan rebel named Hugo Chavez
You should have seen him launching his offense
Telling the whole world at the United Nations
That he could clearly see
The Devil realized in me
And among all world nations

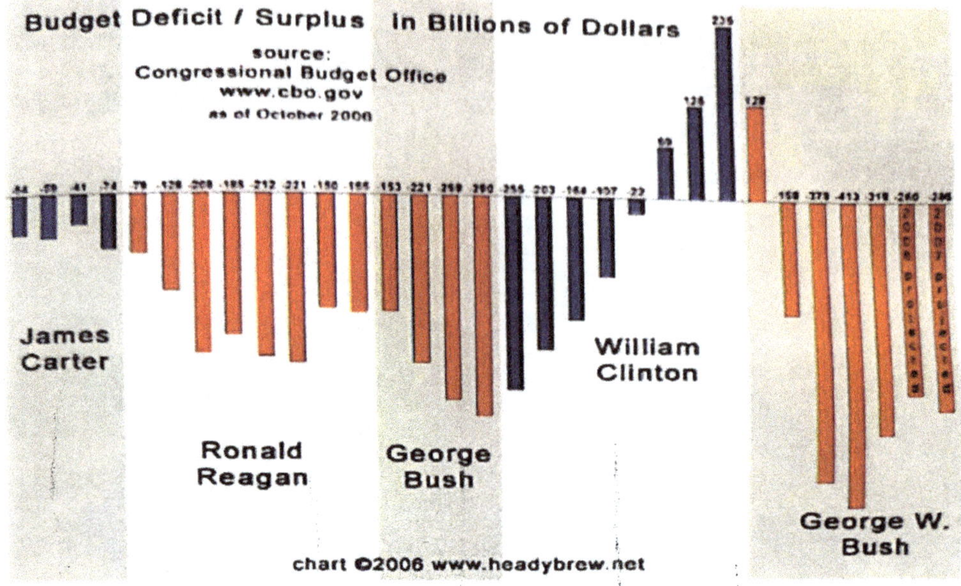

And just like Dad like son
My eight years added more fun
As I left our beloved Country
In borderline depression
From both me and my dad
That is our valuable tradition
For we are descendants of the financiers' elite
Our Machiavelli style is to govern by deceit
Starting the twenty first century
With America's banking system
In near total bankruptcy
And just about to die
With Wall Street crashing
Like the end of the world was nigh
And before any further Bush bushing
Please don't ask me why?
One last days of my dynasty crashing
And just like a Divine Calling
Suddenly the sky was falling?

An artist's portrayal of the state of affairs following the invasion of Iraq by the joint military forces of the United States and Great Britain, or what I call the Pax Ameritanica "virtual empire." The artwork shows the head chef, President George W. Bush, focusing Americas's attention on Saddam Hussein's head as he takes pride in offering it to the American people on the platter as "the big trophy," but the gathered American people are mourning their head and comforting their wounded, while back in the kitchen Donald Rumsfeld, the second U.S. Government Official in command of the war on Iraq, is slicing the pie (in post-Saddam Iraq) with a knife in his hand dealing out pieces of the pie (symbolizing contract awards) to sole sourced American contractors, besides a few select contractors from the invading so-called "war coalition." Meanwhile the Iraqi oil is gushing in (to America) through a gate with the influx being controlled by the head chef himself, who is also an oil man. The deceitful acts here are camouflaged by turning Americans' manageable fear of terror into an unmanageable terror of fear, while the former United States President, Franklin D. Roosevelt, shown at the bottom of the cartoon is turning over in his grave, to no one's surprise, sensing the pending danger (Artwork: by Nabawia Jane El-Soudani, California Institute of the Arts)

U.S. Congressman Henry Waxman Pleaded with President George W. Bush to Review the CIA Evidence and the Case for War, which to Him Clearly Appeared to be Based on Hoax, Primarily Via British Intelligence Sources within the Employ of British Prime Minister Tony Blair.

Regrettably the first preemptive war in American history has already taken place in Iraq commencing on March 19th, 2003, and as of this writing this war has consumed more than half a trillion dollars of the American taxpayers funds, with no end in sight. In a letter, of which excerpts are given below, California Democratic Congressman and Minority Leader, Henry Waxman wrote that letter to President George W. Bush, shortly before the launching of the second Gulf war on Iraq, imploring him to look again at the evidence from the Central Intelligence Agency (CIA) on the alleged Iraqi "weapons of mass destruction" (WMD), which to such an upright and honest Congressman, the alleged evidence appeared to be Hoax. His point was this: Since the United States Central Intelligence Agency, or CIA operatives themselves questioned the validity of what was apparently British-fabricated information (under the Blair Prime Ministry), it was clearly unreliable. With this in mind Congressman Waxman began expressing America's concern to President George W. Bush in his seven page letter of March 17,2003 of which we only present here his introductory remarks as follows:

Dear Mr. President:

I am writing regarding a matter of grave concern. Upon your order, our armed forces will soon initiate the first preemptive war in our nation's history. The most persuasive justification for this in war is that we must act to prevent Iraq from developing nuclear weapons.

That was indeed a very long Good-bye
With best wishes to you all
As today both Laura and I
Are moving to Texas
To our everlasting glory
To a Presidential Library
With million copies of my book
Telling my own story

There will be no such nonsense
About the two stolen elections
For it was sore losing Democrats
Who fabricated such fictions

So I became the first ever U.S. President of
sixteen words
Yet with me Americans were safer than with
Democratic nerds
I performed my oath of Office to perfection with
nothing to hide
So I told sixteen words to a Congress coming
along for the ride
They gave me dozens of standing ovations
and applause
For how timely I rang the bell of nuclear threat
I suppose
All in all sixteen words, and that was all I had
to expose
And that is how I sent Saddam and his nation to
blazing Hell

Crony Capitalism In Control of America
(a Trademark of Three Generations of the Bushes)

Prescott Bush, a United States Senator (1951) / Financier

The Bush Family Descendants of The Financiers' Elite

Definition of Crony Capitalism:

Crony Capitalism = Deal Making, Rainmaking, or Direct Influence Brokerage for Select Enterprises (e.g. Enron, Haliburton, …) with Such Favors to be Returned to the *Influential Deal Makers in Financial Terms.*

The Bounty Hunters and the Hunted

The Hunters

The Hunted

Saddam Hussein, The
Former President of Iraq
before His Hanging
In the Wake of the Invasion of
Iraq Ordered in March 2003
by the United States
President George W. Bush.

The Hunted

Manuel Noriega, The Former
Ruler of Panama Currently
Imprisoned in the United
States of America In the
wake of the Invasion of
Panama Ordered in the Late
1980's by the United States
President George H. W. Bush.

I WANT YOU Never again to vote
Crony Capitalists into public
office: Not in the Executive
Branch, and not in the
Legislative or Judicial Branches.
Crony Capitalism in its mildest
form is a Conflict or Interest,
and in its upper extreme it is a
precursor to Fascism.

ABOUT THE AUTHOR

Dr. Sami El-Soudani is an aerospace materials scientist specializing in fracture mechanics and failure analysis and has been engaged for over thirty years in averting failures of aircraft structures for the past 20 years, however, he has been Conducting independent theological and sociological research prompted by regrettable world events clearly showing that failures of the human spirit are of far devastating consequences than failures of aircraft structures. Dr. El-Soudani, was born in Egypt, received his undergraduate degree from the soviet Union, his MSc Degree from Massachusetts Institute of Technology (USA) and his PhD Degree from the University of Cambridge, England.